Please, No Mice!

By Lora Goff

11-4-21

To all the Children who
visit the Library-
Hope you enjoy
the story
Lora Goff

Illustrated by Lizy J. Campbell

Please, No Mice! By Lora Goff

Published by Pen It! Publications, LLC in the United States of America
812-371-4128 www.penitpublications.com

ISBN: 978-1-954868-65-6

Illustrated by Lizy J Campbell

This Book Belongs To

____

Dedication

I would like to dedicate this book to Isaiah, Felicity, Richard, and Bea.

Acknowledgements

A big thank you to all those who encourage me to keep writing. Also, to Pen It! Publications and all those who work so hard to bring it all together.

Miss Posselworth is a sweet little lady who lives just outside of town on Possum Trot Road.

Her house is very old and in need of much repair. All the shutters need painting. The attic window is cracked because someone was hitting baseballs to close to her house. The screen door is hanging loose on its hinges.

But, this doesn't stop Miss Posselworth from planting oodles of daisies, roses, and petunias all around her house.

She loves to sit on the porch and look at her pretty flowers.

That is, until the day she saw a mouse creeping across her porch. That furry little rodent with dark, beady eyes, looked first this way and that way. He wiggled his whiskers, and skittered as quick as lightning under the screen and right into Miss Posselworth's house.

"OH, DRAT!" yelled Miss Posselworth, as she jumped out of her chair.

"THAT WAS A MOUSE AND I DO NOT LIKE MICE!"

"I love horses and sheep and Little Bo Peep, kittens, and puppies, and fast swimming guppies,

But, I don't like furry gray mice!"

"I love cookies, and candy, and cake would be dandy. I like pickles, and carrots, and bright colored parrots.

But, I don't like those cheese-eating mice!"

PICKLES

"I love sunshine, and flowers, and warm summer showers; bluebirds, and finches, and yellow painted benches.

"But, I don't like those long-tailed mice!"

"I love parties, and games, and my best friend, James. I like trucks, and bikes, and long helicopter flights. But I don't like those whiskery mice!"

"I love rockets, and planes, and all kinds of trains.

BUT PLEASE, NO, NO, NO, MICE!"

Miss Posselworth picked up her broom and went after that furry little rodent with the dark, beady eyes.

Will she catch him or will this little gray mouse, that Miss Posselworth doesn't want in her house, find a hole and escape?

What do you think?

The End!

Author Lora Goff was born in a small farming community near Lebanon, Indiana. At two years of age her mother passed away and her life changed dramatically. She moved in with her oldest sister and family. Her love for God at an early age, along with the values she was taught, has influenced her writing.

Lora is a graduate of Indiana University with a Masters in Elementary Education. She retired after teaching for thirty-three years in the public schools. She has taught classes on How to Write Your Life Story/Memoir Writing. She now spends time writing, visiting with those who are homebound and/or in nursing home facilities. She also volunteers at a local hospital, and teaches a weekly in-depth Bible Study at her church.

Lora's writings have been published in *Light From the Word*, a daily devotional of the Wesleyan Publishing House, the *Good Old Days* magazine, as well as articles in the county newspaper. She also writes a daily blog; *Hope in God Devotionals*. This is her second book with Pen It! Publications, LLC. Her first book, *Growing Up With Granny* was published in 2019.

Lora is a member of the Noblesville, Indiana Writer's Group and the Westfield, Indiana Writer's Group.

Lora and her late husband, Rollie, have four grown children, six grandchildren, and two great-grandchildren. She loves writing, music, watching football, walking, and being with family. Lora and her husband, Rex, divide their time between Noblesville, IN and Frankfort, Ky.

CPSIA information can be obtained
at www.ICGtesting.com
Printed in the USA
LVHW072248300821
696518LV00002B/9